BALLOON TOONS®

The TOTALLY AWESOME EPIC QUEST of the BRAVE BOY KNIGHT

by Pranas T. Naujokaitis
colors by Amy Rumbarger

BLUE APPLE BOOKS

THE EPIC QUEST BEGINS
CAN YOU SET THE TABLE FOR BREAKFAST, HONEY?
NO WAY! SETTING THE TABLE IS BORING!
BOY KNIGHTS DON'T SET TABLES!
VROOOOOOM
EXCUSE ME, YOUNG MAN?
NOVEMBER
SORRY, MOM...

IT'S NOT FAIR, BUTTERSCOTCH!
I SHOULDN'T BE SETTING TABLES. I SHOULD BE HAVING EPIC QUESTS!
RUSTLE
EEK!
STAND BACK! IT'S A WILD RACCOON!

I'M NOT A RACCOON, DUDE. I'M THE ANIMAL PRINCESS!
YOU'RE A GIRL!
AND YOU'RE A BOY. SO WHAT?
YUCK!
GACK!

I HAVE A TOTALLY EPIC QUEST FOR TWO BRAVE KNIGHTS.
ARE YOU GUYS IN?
WE ARE TWO BRAVE KNIGHTS. WE ACCEPT.
CLAP CLAP
CLAP
CLAP
COOL. LET ME TELEPORT YOU.
TELE-WHAT?

OW... MY HEAD.
GASP!
WHERE ARE WE?
WELCOME, BRAVE KNIGHTS, TO MY KINGDOM!
DID YOU CHANGE OUTFITS?
UP

BRAVE KNIGHTS, I BROUGHT YOU HERE BECAUSE I NEED YOUR HELP!

THAT GREEN MONSTER IS DESTROYING MY KINGDOM. THAT IS SO UNCOOL.
GRRRRR!
SMASH

LET'S KNOCK THAT GIANT BOOGER DOWN A PEG, BUTTERSCOTCH.
YEAH! LET'S GO!
WOO HOO!
UM...
SKREEEEEECH

THIS GUY IS HUGE!
PUNCH!

AND HE SMELLS LIKE STINKY CHEESE.
YUM!
YUCK!

WATCH OUT! GIANT FIST!
WHOA! CLOSE ONE.
THUD!
THAT IS ONE MEAN GREEN MONSTER.

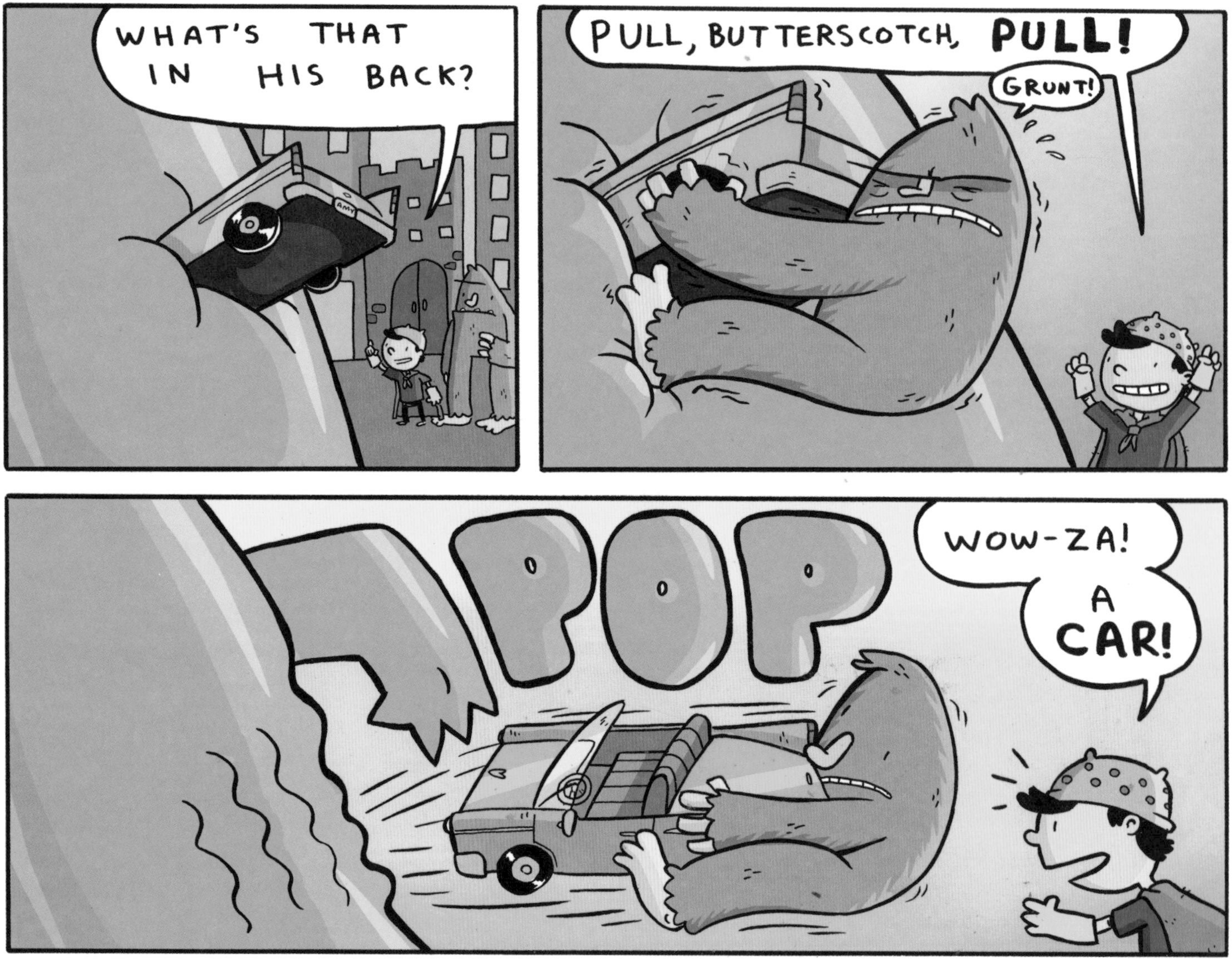
WHAT'S THAT IN HIS BACK?
PULL, BUTTERSCOTCH, PULL!
GRUNT!
POP
WOW-ZA!
A CAR!

GOLLY! WHAT A RELIEF!
THANKS! I'VE BEEN TRYING TO GET THAT CAR OUT FOR WEEKS! IT WAS MAKING ME SUPER CRANKY!
NO PROBLEM.

THANK YOU, BRAVE KNIGHTS.
IT WAS NOTHING.
AND THANK YOU, MONSTER, FOR HELPING PUT THE CITY BACK TOGETHER.
PLEASE, CALL ME HERBERT.
GLUE

SEARCH FOR THE HIDDEN TREASURE
OH BRAVE KNIGHTS, I NEED YOUR HELP.
I'M TOO BUSY PRACTICING MY LASER SWORD MOVES.
VROOOOOOOM
BUT I NEED YOUR HELP FINDING
HIDDEN TREASURE.
HIDDEN TREASURE?
OOOOOH

USE THIS OLD MAP TO FIND IT.
X MARKS THE SPOT.
LET'S ROLL!
GRUNT!
HURRY UP WITH ALL THAT TREASURE-HUNTING GEAR, BUTTERSCOTCH.

WE'RE ALMOST AT THE CAVE.
DO NOT ENTER!

GRUNT!
PFFT! IT DOESN'T LOOK THAT DANGEROUS.
LET'S GO!

HALT, BOY KNIGHT! YOU SHALL NOT PASS.
YEAH!
YIKES!
WE GUARD THIS CAVE. GO AWAY!
YEAH!
NO WAY, SNOT BREATH!
THAT'S NOT A VERY NICE THING TO SAY!
Y... YEAH!

IF YOU'RE GOING TO BE A GIANT MEANIE, THEN WE'RE GOING HOME.
YEAH!
WOW, THAT WAS EASY!

IT SURE IS DARK IN HERE.
LET'S SHED SOME LIGHT ON THE SITUATION.
VROOOOOOM
CLICK
HISSSS
HISSSSS...LEAVE THIS CAVE!
EEK! A BAT DUDE!

STAND BACK!
I HAVE A LASER SWORD!
HA HA HA!
PUH-LEASE! THAT IS ONLY A FANCY TOY FLASHLIGHT!
AGH! MY SUPER-SENSITIVE EYES!
HISSS
SNAP!

GRUMBLE GRUMBLE
OK, LET'S KEEP GOING.
CLICK
LOOK! AN OPENING!
GASP!
THE HIDDEN TREASURE

I WONDER WHAT'S INSIDE!

MONEY?
RUBIES?
SPACE DUDES
CUPCAKES?
SUPER-RARE ACTION FIGURES?

CREEEEEEAK

SURPRISE!
SMOOOCH!
THE TREASURE IS A KISS FROM ME!
YUCK! WORST HIDDEN TREASURE EVER!
HEE HEE!
HA HA!

KNIGHTS ON PATROL
WE HAVE TO PATROL THE KINGDOM.
WE HAVE TO KEEP IT SAFE FROM MONSTERS!
IT IS OUR DUTY AS BRAVE KNIGHTS!
RUSTLE
WHAT'S THAT?

IT'S PROBABLY JUST THE ANIMAL PRINCESS TRYING TO SCARE US AGAIN.
WINK
I HOPE THAT NO ONE JUMPS OUT OF THESE BUSHES AND SCARES US!
RUSTLE
A-HA! GOT YA!
NO ONE'S HERE!
GRUNT?

HMM...
ME-OW
ACK!
IT'S JUST A SMELLY CAT.
MEOW MEOW!
HMM... WHERE COULD THE PRINCESS BE?

ME-OW
AGH!

GOT YA!
HEH HEH!
HEE HA HA HA HEE HEE HA HA HA HA HA HA
BEING A BRAVE BOY KNIGHT IS **VERY** HARD WORK.

AFTER A BUSY DAY IT IS TIME FOR BED
GOOD NIGHT, BUTTER-SCOTCH.
MOM, I'M HOME.
DID YOU HAVE A GOOD DAY PLAYING, SWEETIE?
I HAD SO MANY EPIC ADVENTURES. THERE WERE MONSTERS AND CAVES AND HIDDEN TREASURE!

AND TOMORROW YOU'LL HAVE EVEN MORE ADVENTURES.
KISS
GOOD NIGHT, MY BRAVE BOY KNIGHT
GOOD NIGHT, MOM.
4

Z
THE END